Michael outstretched his great big wings, which covered the surrounding area with a plethora of feathers. Then with a single swoop he leapt masterfully into the sky. Soon he was above the buildings, crossing the city as if he were a part of the wind itself.

The training hall was near, so he was there in mere moments. Relaxing his wings he landed swiftly. And as he had done many times before, he reached for the door and opened it, entering the great training room.

HEAVEN'S BLADE

WHEN DESTINY CALLS

by

J.S. MILIK

FOR MY WIFE, CRYSTAL, WHO BELIEVES IN ME;
AND FOR MY MOTHER, BROTHER, AND FATHER,
WHO ADVISE ME AND SUPPORT MY WORK.

Published by
Universal Works Publishing

ISBN: 978-0-578-45046-9

Contents

*Destiny is a funny thing; for some strive hard to reach theirs,
while others it comes up from behind and bites them,
like a snake in the grass you never see.*

HEAVEN'S BLADE

WHEN DESTINY CALLS

Prologue

The city of Heaven is the biggest city in all existence. Even down town is greater than all the cities of Earth put together. The land is made of clouds, and the sky is always blue. In the center of the city is a massive temple, the temple of God. Supposedly God sits on a throne in there, but not many angels have been.

At the outskirts of the city, there are many mountains made out of clouds and a plain that leads to infinity. You may see some angels wandering about this area, pondering existence, or having fun flying around with their huge dove wings. There are many towns in heaven, but none as grand as the big city. Each building is made with a unique quality, some made of crystal, some made of marble, while others seem to be made from the very cloud they sit upon.

Within Heaven there are over one hundred thousand angels, and there are over a million souls (released from their bodily form). They all exist for-ever and ever. This is God's will.

In the streets of the big city, it is quite a sight. Most of the souls are very intelligent, having been given access to the Heavenly Library for thousands of years. But there are a few who are new there. With astonished eyes, they look like tourists. So many things to do, so many celebrities to see (Adam, Eve, Noah, Moses, etc . . .).

This was a time in Heaven's history that was very majestic, before the darkness, before Hell itself was created.

CHAPTER I

The Sword, the Gate, and the Author

Now the angel Michael was just an average angel at the time, not much to his name at all really. He had done a few tasks for God in the past, but even so, most angels had done much more than him. In fact angels were called down to Earth by God all the time.

Michael thought about how the angel Gabriel

was sent down to Earth recently to make sure that lions would not eat some poor chap. "I must admit I have a little bit of envy," he said to himself, "but not enough to be sinful, of course," he added. He had been a servant of God's for three thousand years, and still he did not feel special.

He continued to sit on his cloud couch thinking about the past. The white robe he wore did not stand out at all against the couch. Now you might think this couch as strange considering the time it was on Earth (humans did not invent couches yet), but comfort was very important in Heaven.

When he stood up, great white eagle shaped wings could be seen folded on his back. He then strode across the marble floor of his apartment, and stopped to look out of one of his crystal windows. It was time for his sword practice.

Like all sports, sword fighting was meant to be fun. And if you got good enough at blocking you could use real swords, because chances are you would not get hurt. Michael was great at blocking. He had taken-up sword fighting two thousand years ago, and even an idiot would be good at it after that much time.

He picked the sword off the wall with ease, then he left and went outside onto the marble sidewalk. Horses on the road brought color to the city. They were brown, black, and pale. Some of them were pulling carriages and others had humans riding them. Horses rarely kept to themselves. They could be seen mingling with angels and other horses.

Michael outstretched his great big wings, which covered the surrounding area with a plethora of feathers. Then with a single swoop he leapt masterfully into the sky. Soon he was above the buildings, crossing the city as if he were a part of the wind itself.

The training hall was near, so he was there in mere moments. Relaxing his wings he landed swiftly. And as he had done many times before, he reached for the door and opened it, entering the great training room.

Inside lots of angels were fighting each other in

competition. Michael saw his fencing partner instantly.

"Good to see you again Uriel," Michael said, "are you ready?"

"Yes," Uriel answered, "you know I am always ready."

Swinging their swords up they both saluted each other. Their swords could ignite, but that was only for real use, so they fenced with their fires doused. And as their swords clashed, each one thought that they had the upper hand. Michael blocked and then countered with a side strike, but Uriel parried it away. It continued as such, but in the end Uriel struck the final blow to Michael's chest. He staggered a bit, and looked up.

"Amazing, I can never beat you!" Michael said in a gasp.

"Well, I have been doing this sport for a few hundred more years than you," Uriel said, more to himself than to Michael.

Michael stood closer, his wound already healed. "You must be the best," Michael stated.

"No, you forget, Satan is unmatched," Uriel pointed out.

"I can't believe you lost to him," Michael said, trying to make sense of the whole thing.

"Shall we go get something to eat?" Uriel suggested, sliding his sword into his belt.

"Yes, sounds good," Michael replied, holding back his wish for another round.

They both left and took off from the side walk, flying side by side looking for their favorite restaurant.

The restaurant they looked for was a quaint little place made out of a strange cloud material that people up there had mastered the use of.

After spotting the restaurant they both landed and went inside. The chef was a human who loved to cook so much that now he does it in Heaven, just for fun. Harp music played quietly in the background (for some strange reason all angels liked harp music).

They decided to sit at a table near the window. This was their favorite seat. Now, angels and humans did not have to eat in Heaven because they always were their right weight. Instead eating was for fun and enjoyment only.

Then the chef came. Uriel ordered rice, while Michael decided upon mash potatoes. This was their usual choice of food.

A thought crossed Michael's mind. "So why do you think Satan is so good?"

Uriel was surprised at the question, but quickly figured out what he was talking about. "Oh, you mean at fencing. Well he's been doing it for as long as we have, and he seems to enjoy it more than us."

"He has a big responsibility, being the most powerful angel," Uriel added as Michael started to eat his potatoes.

Michael thought about how the flaming swords have been used in the past—a single swing while ablaze would destroy a whole city, or instill fear in many towns at once. Those tactics had not been used for a thousand years. People like Moses, King Solomon, and Alexander the Great helped transform the world. Human civilization on Earth was not as barbaric and did not need to be tamed in such ways.

"Sword fighting has no practical use for us angels anymore," Michael expressed.

"I know what you mean, but what is your point?" Uriel inquired.

"It's just, how does he have the time for such a sport?" Michael wondered, thinking about all the responsibilities a leader like Satan had to deal with.

"Quite frankly it does seem a little out of the ordinary, maybe you should ask him sometime," Uriel said.

"No, that's okay," Michael said, with certainty in his eyes.

Michael only saw Satan once in a while, but he always had to build up his courage to speak to such a high ranking angel. Satan was the head of all the angels in Heaven, and so he was famous and held a lot of authority. What if Michael said something wrong? How could he exist with himself after that?

A human stranger entered the restaurant. He

looked like a thirty year old, but almost all people in Heaven feel best at that age, so it was no surprise. "Where am I?" he said with a confused look on his face.

Michael glanced a look at Uriel. "It's another new one," he said.

The man wandered over to the table, crinkling his face. He still put on his old man look, from which he had when he died. "The last thing I remember I was shearing some sheep and . . . wait . . . I was choking on some wool." His hand went to his throat as if he still had it in there and his mouth gaped open in shock.

"I would have thought a guy like him would have died of natural causes," Uriel said.

"Well, you can never be too sure," Michael said, now smiling. "Please sit down. Can I offer you a drink?" Michael was being as courteous as possible.

"I'm in heaven aren't I?" the man said, sitting down at the table.

"You got it," Michael said.

"You're both angels?"

"Correct. You're really catching on," answered Michael.

There was a small pause as the stranger was taking it all in . . . cloud walls, crystal windows, and two winged people sitting at the table with him.

"Wool, what a way to go," Uriel uttered.

The stranger broke a smile, and then started laughing, "Yes it certainly was."

It was contagious, and soon everyone at the table was laughing also.

After the laughter calmed, Michael declared, "I knew you were a good spirited fellow when you came in here."

"You did?" The man's expressions finally fit in with his new age. "Can you tell me more? What kinds of things go on up here?"

Michael was quick to respond. "Well, you don't have to worry about death anymore. Food can't kill you—it is always good for you."

"And when you go swimming in the Heavenly Lakes you do not have to worry about drowning," Uriel continued.

"But the most important thing is that you can't die from choking on wool," Michael said with an understanding grin.

The man appreciated Michael's concern, and smiled in return.

"You know what, you should go to see Zephon," Uriel decided.

"Yes, good suggestion," Michael said, excited for the man. "The librarian in the Heavenly Library is a great angel. He can teach you what you need to know."

The man was happy to hear of this library and was instantly excited. "Well, I best be on my way then."

"Yes, keep in touch," Michael said as the man left the table.

Michael never got tired of meeting new people. Heaven always seemed more lively with them around.

Then the man past by a women angel who was just entering the restaurant. Her beauty lit the man's face brighter than it already was—and he strode out the door.

The angel walked over to their table, and looked over at Uriel. Her wings were more like a dove's wings than Michael's. This was because she was a women angel, and women angel's wings differ from that of a man angel's wings. Be not surprised that her dove wings just added to her pure loveliness.

"Hello Gabriel," Uriel said, with a smile.

"Yes, what do you want?" Michael asked, suspicious of her intent. Gabriel's loveliness would not put him under a spell; he knew that she came strictly for business purposes.

"Uriel, Satan needs you to go on a mission," Gabriel said.

"Needed by the boss again?" Michael wondered, a little perturbed.

"Well, he needs someone to go down to Earth and save a general who is about to be assassinated," Gabriel explained.

"Is there any chance my friend Michael can go with me this time?" Uriel suggested.

"No, I'm afraid only one is needed and you've done this kind of job before," Gabriel explained.

"Then why aren't you doing this job, Gabriel?" Michael broke in, trying to get the upper hand in the matter.

"I have my own mission I'm doing. This was just on my way," Gabriel said looking Michael in the eyes.

This got under Michael's wings, why should she be so high and mighty, ordering angels around like she owns the place.

"I'm sure I won't be long," Uriel said to Michael.

Uriel got up, and then they both left. They were on their way to Heaven's gate, so that once again they would step down the ladder to the physical realm.

Michael smirked a bit, realizing he was alone again. Uriel was his only friend in Heaven, and he had known him for a thousand years. In fact, nobody else knew each other better than these two.

Other friends in the past just left him—it was like nobody else cared. But when everyone else was gone, Uriel, his best friend, remained.

Shortly after he finished his potatoes he left as well, and walked down the street. There were many people on the street, and horses could once again also be seen. But even with this commotion he noticed an angel in the sky coming down at him.

Michael backed up and saw the angel land in front of him. It was Jahoel, known as the messenger of God—he had visited God more than any other angel, and it was evident in his eyes. He had a light brown beard, and a holy sword by his side.

Michael was of course surprised to see him. "What's wrong? Is there a problem with one of your kids?"

Michael said this because Jahoel was also in charge of the Child School, which was a place where children who died young would go to learn what they did not get the chance to on Earth.

"No, I have word from God. You are to go to him," said Jahoel.

"Right now?!?" Michael asked, continuing to be surprised.

"Yes," Jahoel replied.

What could this be about? Michael thought. He felt awkward at first—it was a little out of the ordinary, and it took him a second to realize the importance of his duty.

"Oh, and Michael, remember to set your sword ablaze in honor of your meeting," Jahoel added.

Michael, hearing this, turned and pulled his sword from its scabbard. It then ignited instantly, and as he raised the sword over his head he spread open his wings and took off.

He flew above the city with only one goal in his mind, to approach God.

He then landed with a graceful thud, quickly wrapping his wings to his back. Sword still in hand he slowly walked to the entrance way of the central building (the temple of God).

With a thought, the sword slowly extinguished its flames, making visible the words, 'EX CAELO' on its blade.

He then leaned the blade against the opening and entered.

Michael entered a long white marble hallway with an open door at the other end. This short journey always excited him, even in his dreams.

He walked the hallway slowly as to remember each and every step, then passing through the doorway he entered the great room.

Naturally, the first thing his eye caught was God, sitting on his throne at the head of a great table covered with many books. Also known as the Lord Almighty, he or she (as some might say) was one of many forms and many places. But this time he took the form of a man, about angel size.

Other chairs surrounded the table, some had name plates on them: Jesus, Holy Spirit, Moses, Ezekiel. Michael recognized some but not all. They must have been away doing business of some kind or another. But one thing became certainly clear to Michael, it was just him and God this time.

The Lord made a hand gesture to Michael telling him that he could sit.

After kneeling on one knee, he sat in one of the chairs. Then he could see who wrote all the books on the table: 'The Book of Life' by God, 'The Book of Truth' by God, 'The book of the Way' by God, (these were just some of the titles).

"It is an honor to be called here," Michael said cautiously.

"Yes . . . I need your help," God replied with a half smile.

This was the last thing Michael thought God would say, and he was even more shocked that it was the first words out of the Lord Almighty's mouth.

God continued, "as you know there is a delicate balance in the universe. That is why I am not going to use my power to help you. You see, people would lose their respect for me."

"How can that be?!?" Michael exclaimed.

"You know it is true, and so you will have to fight the war yourself."

"A war?" he said, retracting in shock.

"Yes, there will be a war, and you will have to lead the angels into battle."

Michael thought for a second. A *war had never happened in Heaven—it was always a place of peace.*

"How can I do this?" Michael asked in a softer voice.

"You know all you need to. Serve me well, for all of existence hangs in the balance." These words seemed to enter Michael's eyes rather than his ears, as Michael envisioned Heaven crumbling to pieces.

Michael stood in a hurry, almost forgetting where he was. He knelt and left, knowing only what he must do.

When he left the building, he stopped dead in his tracks. He almost forgot his sword. Bending down he grabbed its hilt. The blade was dragged along the ground as he brought it toward him. Maybe it was to sharpen the blade, but what it really was for—was to hear the sound that would soon fill the skies as war raged on in Heaven.

CHAPTER II

The Way to Heaven's Park

Soon after that Michael was in the skies looking for his friend Uriel. And with a quick landing at the golden gates, he waited. Two guards were stationed on either side of the gate, and their eyes questioned Michael's intent. Then in mere moments his friend went through the gates to enter Heaven.

Michael was the first to speak. "Uriel, I need to tell you something."

"What is it?" Uriel answered, not expecting to see his friend. "Can't you let me settle back in first?"

"This can't wait," Michael said. "I need to talk to you in private."

Seeing the concern on his friend's face, Uriel knew at once it was serious, so without another question, he left with Michael.

Although Uriel's apartment was closer, they did not go there because it was a crystal apartment; those could be seen through much easier than any other kind. Instead they flew to the city park.

Of all the places in the city, the park was the most beautiful. Pink, red, and green trees surrounded the park, while purple and white flowers were all around. Marble brick walkways and crystal clear ponds sparkled throughout the park as well. It was a purely peaceful place.

Michael was worried about the whole situation

and really needed his friend's council—this above all stood out in his mind.

They both walked along with their heads bowed, contemplating what each other might say. "I was just in a meeting with God." Michael finally revealed, sure that no one else could hear.

"You were?" Uriel's face showed confusion all about it.

"He wants me to lead an angel army, I am to save Heaven."

"Oh, you're joking," Uriel concluded, because a war in Heaven was preposterous.

"No, I'm not!" Michael said, continuing to look serious.

"Really? You're serious?"

"Yes!"

The two of them stopped for a second after that comment. It finally started to sink in that Michael had bitten off more than he could chew.

Uriel was concerned about his friend. "Why didn't you refuse? Shouldn't Satan be doing this, I mean even I am more qualified to lead an army than you are?"

It did not even cross Michael's mind, but Uriel was right—Satan should lead his own army.

"I know you're right, but God said I am the one, and he would know better than any one else," Michael reasoned.

Uriel thought for a second. "You know it is funny you should say that, because lately the missions I've been sent on by Satan have been a little strange," Uriel pointed out.

Michael gave a puzzled look when he heard this. "What do you mean?"

"For example, the General I just saved on Earth was actually a warlord—with a very destructive intent, I might add," Uriel explained.

"Well, maybe Satan is getting unreliable information lately. That would explain why he is not to lead our army in this upcoming war," Michael said, trying to make sense of the whole matter.

"Wow, this means—he'll be under your command," Uriel said.

"You're right," Michael said, finally realizing how important he really was.

They stopped on a bridge overlooking a pond. The blue sky glistened on the water, and fish could be seen swimming about.

"I'm going to need more training. Tell me what your secret is. How can I be as great as you are with a sword?" Michael asked.

"I suggest you go to the library," answered Uriel.

"But how is that useful? Knowing and doing are completely different." Michael had many experiences in the past trying to learn new moves from books and he always failed.

"You're right, but you know the basics. And the secret of learning techniques from a book, is to look up what you already know, and then pay attention to the style of the book. When you know the style, then the new comes naturally," Uriel stated, making evident his thousand year old wisdom.

Michael was wondering what to do next. He could study in the library while the forces of both sides were gathering together, but that might not be the best move to make.

"Well, I suggest we should seek out Satan," Uriel Said. "He has more powers than other angels and we need to get him on our side right away. What do you think?"

"Yes, that is a good idea. Lets go," said Michael, not quite sure what 'powers' Uriel was referring to.

CHAPTER III

Unexpected Guests

While Michael and Uriel were having their meeting in the park, Satan also was having a meeting of his own.

Satan was in his marble mansion talking to the angel, Azael. Big pillars surrounded the huge room, and not a window was in sight. Satan loved his privacy. The things he could do without prying eyes made him feel more powerful.

"What next Master?" Azael asked Satan.

"Don't speak unless you're spoken to!" Satan said, lowering his brow.

"Sorry—"

"You should be! You're a waste of wings you know," Satan said.

Satan was under a lot of pressure, but he dealt with it in his own personal way. And Azael being his main subordinate took the brunt of it.

"If you must know, I will stop the chaos in the universe, and it is quite easy. You see, God is wrong. People don't need freedom—they are quite content with just following orders," Satan said with a smile. "I will add ten more commandments down on Earth, and in Heaven I will be dictator."

"How will God let you do this?" Azael wondered out loud.

"You lazy halfwit. Don't you know that if God interfered he would lose all his political power and would have to start creation from scratch again. You know as well as me that wingless slug would dare not do such a thing."

Satan was right about that. He had met with God almost as much as Jahoel and knew what existence was all about, more than any other angel. Perhaps it was his deep interest that caused him to find so many things he personally disagreed with.

"With everyone's free will in check there can be no problems—there will be order!" Satan added. A smile struck his face as he thought of his great idea.

"I know better than any—God is unfit to rule," said Azael, resting his hands on the two swords by his sides.

"You bet. The way that all-powerful oaf trapped you in a cave—it was a disgrace," Satan agreed.

"A thousand year sentence for a little mischief!" Azael stated, getting excited about Satan's plans.

"God's feelings toward people are beginning to sicken me. Perhaps we would all be better off if they were completely obliterated."

Azael smiled.

Satan continued, "Every week I have to do some messed up job, teaching some people a lesson about life on Earth. I am tired of it . . . People live on

Earth for less than a century. God is wasting my time and my power. I have had enough of his love of man and his tolerance of them. What a moron!"

Just then Michael and Uriel knocked on the door. Azael answered and let them in!

Needing a second to build up his courage, Michael spoke, "Satan . . . I have come because I need your help."

"You do?" Satan answered, suspiciously.

"There is a war coming and you should be on our side, to help me," Michael said, shaking a little.

"A war? Well, if I am leading the army, then yes," said Satan.

"God said I should lead," said Michael, beginning to get a bad feeling.

"God?" Satan retracted in suspicion. "Ahh, I see, but I don't need a war to take over." Satan was quite sure he could have ruled without a fight, I mean who would dare fight Satan, lord of all angels, and the greatest sword master ever?

Michael retracted also, but this was more from shock than suspicion.

"What is going on here?" Uriel said, a bit confused.

"Heaven will soon be under my rule, Uriel, and you and your angel here will serve under me, like you always have," Satan explained, having already planned it all out thoroughly in his mind.

"He is not 'my angel', he is my friend Michael," Uriel said.

"I think I've seen him around before, but he is a pathetic little angel. Why God wants him to lead an army—only shows how foolish he has become," Satan answered.

"Hey, watch it!" Michael said, a little insulted.

"God is the creator of the universe. Why do you dare defy him?" said Uriel.

"Just because someone created something does not mean he knows how to take care of it," Satan stated.

"Who better to know a creation, than its own creator!" Michael, snapped back, infuriated at Satan's ideas.

"We could go on about this forever," Satan said,

"the fact is, with me in charge, I would be the all-powerful one—and you could have whatever you want under my rule, Michael. Just come to my side." Satan then gestured to Michael.

"You're crazy, this is not the way it is meant to be," Michael said. "Where is the balance in that?"

"Balance never existed. It is a pipe dream." Satan thought about all the disorder in the universe and how sloppy it seemed to him.

Uriel chimed in, "You are a fool. Peace is balance—and that is what it is all about."

Satan pulled out his sword, and set it ablaze. "If you are against me, then why should you exist?"

Uriel pulled out his sword to defend himself—soon it was glowing as well. He did not stand a chance against Satan, this much was certain—but he couldn't just give up, there was too much at stake.

Satan approached Uriel as Azael pulled out both of his swords, bringing them to Michael's neck, to keep him in check. Then Satan struck at Uriel, but the blade clashed with the flames on

Uriel's. Uriel then struck at Satan's head but it also was parried away. The battle continued, and then Satan, swung his blade down, and then up and around, Uriel was able to block that, but he could not block the spin and stab which came right after it. The flames of Satan's sword went right through Uriel's back, causing him to collapsed onto the marble floor.

Uriel only thought of how he failed his friend. The anguish and pain he felt was intense.

Michael had never seen an angel fall in such a way. In fact he had never seen or heard of an angel being struck by a flaming sword. Uriel's wound did not heal!

Michael was shocked at first, but when Uriel's blood seeped out and dripped on the floor, his shock turned to fury. "WHAT!!! NOOO! THIS CAN'T BE?!?" Michael, could not stand the thought of losing his best friend. But then he fell silent as Uriel managed to say one last word: "M-M-Michael . . ."

Satan laughed. "What a fool," he said looking at

Uriel. "You know I could not have such a powerful sword master working against me."

Michael drew his sword and set it afire so fast that it was as if it was always at the ready. But Azael continued to point two swords at his throat, taunting his every desire for vengeance.

"Let him come," Satan said to Azael.

Azael dropped his swords and got out of the way.

Michael charged in with a strike, but it was parried away, and then Satan swung around Michael and struck him in the chest. Michael fell to the floor. This chest wound would never heal, Michael knew. Then Satan knelt down and used the other end of his sword to pummel Michael in the head. Michael was now knocked unconscious.

"He should be dead shortly. Throw him outside," Satan ordered to Azael.

"What about the war, is it a crock of scum?" Azael said.

"Moron! Did that cave make you go mental? The

war is inevitable—these two were against us, so there will be more losers just like them," Satan replied.

Shortly after that, Michael had a terrible dream; war was coming and he was no where to be found. Satan's angels were everywhere, and darkness filled the skies. Then God disappeared and his temple crumbled to the clouds.

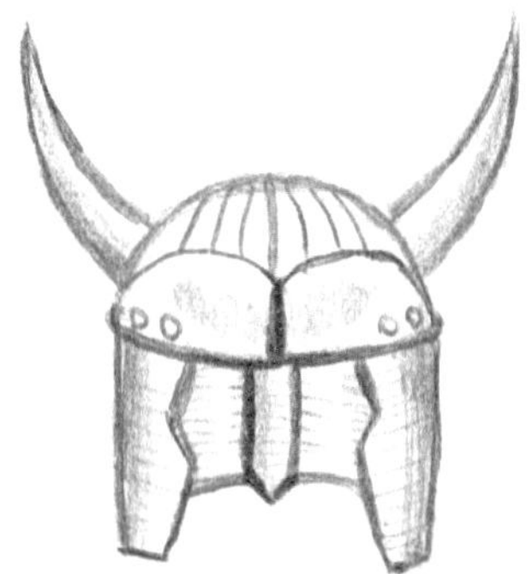

The Helmet From Above

Michael woke and he saw a familiar face. It was Raphael, the angel in charge of healing on Earth. Michael looked around, he was in Raphael's house, the place where people and angels come if they are injured in Heaven. There were only five injuries in the past millennium that needed medical attention in Heaven. Now there were two more.

The walls of Raphael's house were made of the

most reflective white marble. Michael sat up on the bed he was on and looked at his reflection in the wall. He pulled his robe to the side to see the scar.

"What happened?" Raphael said.

"I was cut in the chest by a flaming sword." Michael pulled the robes back over his chest.

"I have never seen such a thing before. Your friend, was he stabbed by one?" Raphael asked.

"Uriel, what happened to him?" Michael quickly wanting an answer.

"I'm sorry . . . he's gone." Raphael was cautious. He never had to tell an angel such bad news before.

"He's Dead?!? How Can This Be?!?" Michael tried to calm down. Breathing heavy, he had a worried look on his face. He longed for another chance to say something to his friend.

"I don't know how this happened. There's never been a death in Heaven before," Raphael explained.

"Can I see his body?" Michael whispered. He thought about all the loneliness he would soon have now that his good friend was gone. He was like family.

"It was here, but it slowly faded away, and now it is gone," Raphael answered, worried about his patient.

This was different than anything Michael had ever heard about.

"What about me?" Michael was scared for a second.

"You will always have a scar on your chest, but other than that you should be fine," Raphael reassured him.

Michael got up. "I have things I must do." Then it hit him—the aftermath of the war would not be a pretty one. "You may be very busy soon, and I feel for you."

Michael left Raphael with that last thought. And after he got outside he left the street for the sky. As he flew, he had to set aside what was in his heart, for destiny called. Gabriel was walking far below, and so he decided to land.

"Gabriel, please help me," Michael said.

"You need '*my*' help?" she said, with a puzzled look on her face.

"Yes, Satan has killed Uriel."

"What are you talking about? That makes no sense," Gabriel said, shaking her head in disbelief.

"I know, but think about it. Satan has been acting strange lately—he wants to take over," Michael said, wondering what she might be thinking.

Gabriel thought about Satan's actions lately and they were indeed questionable. In fact Satan himself convinced an army to go against another, resulting in 700 deaths. "Satan killed your friend? I knew it. . . he's finally gone mad," she said in realization.

"The Lord has put me in charge of stopping him," Michael explained. "I need you, Gabriel. You know the angels of Heaven really well, and are a natural leader."

Something inside Gabriel made her feel very guilty at that moment—it was not just the fact that she had served Satan so loyally, but it was the fact that Michael appreciated Gabriel for her talent, and she had always ignored him.

"I need an army of angels to fight in God's name," Michael asked.

"I will see what troops I can get," Gabriel responded without question.

"I need to do something for a couple of days, but I will return," Michael pointed out.

"I will be waiting for you with your army when you return." Gabriel wondered what Michael would be doing, but she knew it must be important.

Michael whipped through the sky looking for the library. He remembered what Uriel told him, 'when you know the style, then the new comes naturally.' It was up to him now, he had to last through the battle, or the angels would lose their general.

It was easy to spot one of the biggest buildings in Heaven, and Michael landed gracefully in front of the great marble door. He strode inside and folded his wings in.

Michael walked up to the front desk in the library. Zephon, the librarian was sitting behind it.

Zephon was an angel with a book always in his hand. A gold band he wore on his head, and he greeted Michael with a smile.

"Zephon, I'm looking for fencing information," Michael said.

"That's great!" Zephon said excitedly. "I like fences too! They are perfect for privacy and keeping unwanted people or angels away. I love fences."

"No, I mean the sword fighting kind of fencing," Michael corrected.

"Oh, you mean that graceful hack and slash stuff, I love that kind of thing!" he said, just as excited.

Zephon lead Michael to that section in the library, and Michael sat down there for hours on end, every once in a while getting up to practice sword techniques. There were others in the library but they were very quiet and did not mind Michael's strange behavior. He found a book called 'Sword Masters: techniques of the blade' by Raziel. He did just as his friend said—looking up the basics he knew, so that the advanced would be clear. It was hard to concentrate at first, having just lost his best friend, but he knew God had a purpose for everything, and that meant his friend did not die in vain.

Michael knew what he was up against, angels could die in Heaven, and Satan was the greatest swordsmen with lots of power. Michael picked up another book called 'Powers of Angels' by Gallizur.

When he left the library forty hours later he had improved greatly, but was it enough? He had lived for thousands of years and he had never learned so much in such a short time before. He could only hope he knew enough to survive.

When Michael flew above the city he saw something he had never seen before—a huge army at the edge of the city—an army of angels. Michael glanced over the mountains and saw another army of angels, this time on the plains. Michael landed at the edge of the city. Gabriel approached, her dove wings opened behind a glimmering suit of armor.

"Your army is ready," she said.

Sure enough every angel had armor, a shield, and a sword.

"There is your armor and shield, Michael," Gabriel added, pointing to a pile of equipment.

"Thank you, Gabriel" Michael said, "This is a great job you've done, and I appreciate it."

"One more thing, Michael. I have come across another angel sword master. His name is Zadkiel," Gabriel found that angel among the troops a few hours earlier, and he was practicing the sword so well that a small audience gathered to watch.

"Yes, I remember Uriel saying something about him once. Okay, Gabriel, I want you and Zadkiel to be my colonels," said Michael, very sure of himself.

Gabriel needed to let something out. "I have great respect for you Michael, and I am really sorry I ignored you all these years."

Michael, hearing this, felt more important than ever, and he felt stronger and better inside because of it.

"Thank you, I needed that." Michael held in his happy emotions, to keep his dignity in front of his angels.

After putting on his armor and shield, he walked through the crowd of angels taking a good look at them. There were many famous angels that had joined his army: Arcan, Oriel, and Mediat were just some of them. As Michael walked on more, he noticed even Jahoel was there.

"Jahoel, you don't have to be here," Michael said to God's most important messenger.

"Angels and humans alike need to fight for what they believe in," Jahoel explained.

Michael understood and he continued to walk, knowing that their loyalty to God was great. The energy and emotion of the angels could be felt in the air. It was time for Michael to give a speech to his angels.

"Fellow angels," Michael voiced as for all to hear, "the time has arrived, and like most of you, I never thought something such as this would happen, but it has. God has given us all free will, and evil was bound to come out of it, but there is still hope. As Gabriel probably told you, I was in a meeting with the Lord Almighty himself about this very matter . . ."

Some of the crowd looked at each other in astonishment. "So it's true?" one of them whispered.

"He told me that this war would determine the outcome of all existence. It is my belief that this war depends on every single one of us, and a single victory could change the tide in our favor . . ."

The whole army was listening carefully to every word Michael said.

Michael continued, "We will not give up our freedom! We will not give up our equality! And we will not give up on our creator!"

"Yeah!" The angels shouted.

"Satan thinks he can pull the wool over our eyes, he thinks he can get the best of us! Well I won't stand for it!"

"Yeah!!"

"I am going to march over that hill, and when

he sees me, still alive, he will kick himself for it. Are you with me!?!" Michael boomed.

"Yeah!!!" the angels shouted, and then they started to march behind Michael.

Meanwhile, Satan was giving a speech of his own. His head was crowned with a horned helmet which made him stand out in the crowd, mostly because very few helmets were worn at this war (angels had unseen halos that protected their heads, of course some say they can see them).

"We will win this war!" Satan yelled. "Those scumbags think they can take away our destiny! I don't think so!" He was not sure what his destiny was, but said it anyways.

"Yeah!" The army shouted, raising their swords to the sky.

"They might have twice as many angels on their side, but they will all die if they stand in my way—I killed Uriel and Michael, so will be the fate of them ALL!!"

"YEAH!!"

"Serve me well, and you will have whatever you

want! Every one of you will own everything you desire, and we will rule the world, finally revealing ourselves to all humans!"

Just then Satan's angels readied themselves and looked to the mountains, as Michael's army came into view.

"It is time . . . Go!" Satan yelled, he wanted to take the other army by surprise.

Angels upon angels took off from the plains and headed for the mountains. Satan noticing Michael was still alive, thought nothing of it and took off into the air himself.

Everything pure and bright was at stake, and Michael could not let Satan's army of darkness extinguish it. In his heart he knew that Satan would fight him, and that they were meant to do this.

Michael shouted to his troops, "Here they come! Defend our city!" Michael pointed his sword toward the angels closing in—and on his command, the angels streaked into the sky.

Legions of angels flew at each other, and then

they clashed over the plains. Heaven rang with the hitting of swords to shields. Michael glided down to the hard as earth clouds of the plains. He felt sure footed there.

Suddenly, four angels landed all around him. They must have been sent by Satan to defeat the leader of their opposition. They attacked from all directions, which was a cleaver idea that would have worked—if it wasn't for the fact that Michael blocked a slash with his shield, another with his sword, and dodged the rest. Bringing his sword around he slashed one, and pummeled another while protecting his side with his shield, which in turn was used as a weapon on the third. A kick to the head knocked out the fourth.

Gabriel came down in distress. "They are fierce up there. My shield was lost in battle already—I need another one," she said.

"Here, take mine. It was only hindering me any-ways," Michael said, handing over his shield. Then he pointed to the sky. "Gabriel, look our lines are breaking. I want you and Zadkiel to lead a surrounding strike to Satan's army."

"Yes, sir," Gabriel said, and flew off.

Just then a horned helmet fell in front of Michael. He looked up and saw Satan fighting high above him. He then put a hand to his armor; the scar on his chest was hidden beneath it. The words 'when you know the style, then the new comes naturally,' filled his mind. He clenched his hand.

Heaven's army would have won already if it was not for Satan. Satan was so skilled at war that even without a shield, he fought a dozen angels at once. This encouraged Satan's army to fight even harder.

Michael raised his flaming sword high. He was a great leader, but he saw that his great army was losing. He needed to do something.

Just then, another angel landed in front of Michael ready to challenge him. It was Azael, his two flaming swords drawn, ready to add Michael to his list of victims.

"Good bye, Michael," Azael said.

Michael dodged one blade as he blocked the other. And as if it was all one fluent motion, Michael stabbed right through the armor. Two swords fell, soon their flames died, much like their master.

"Yes, good bye," Michael said in a cocky reply.

Looking up, Michael focused upon Satan once more, who was continuing to fight off angels, slaying those who got too close.

"Get back! Satan is mine!" Michael commanded.

Angels parted, to make way for their general.

Then he left the plains like lightning leaves a cloud.

KABOOM!!!!! A bright flash temporarily blinded all the angels as Michael's sword clashed with Satan's.

When the light calmed, the war seemed to freeze as thousands watched on to see the outcome of their general. On a nearby hill, even some humans came to watch. Many were shocked at what they saw. Some even wept.

The clash had separated them both for a second.

"You know you will never win," Satan sneered. "Your army is weak."

"Lying snake!" Michael replied. "Lets see what you got."

Satan flew at Michael, sweeping his sword around and up at Michael's ribs, a move that had defeated many. But to his surprise it was parried away. Satan tried again and again with all sorts of fantastic moves, each one with no success.

The infuriated Satan swooped his wings down to rise up while Michael swung his sword and missed. Satan, who was above him now, folded his wings for a dive.

Michael, seeing this, folded his wings in also. But Satan was already diving at him, and the only way for Michael to escape was straight down.

They both fell and Michael needed to act fast. As they fell faster and faster, Michael made a daring move, but he needed to do something. He opened his wings, just before his back would have crashed into the hard surface of the plains.

Satan continued with his downward stab. The stab was greater than any that had ever been done before, and would have killed Michael instantly. But instead of hitting Michael he missed and hit the plains.

The fiery sword resounded as Heaven rumbled—the sword had pierced the plains, and a large crack was formed. Never before had Heaven's floor been cracked.

Enraged, Satan pulled his blade from the ground while he watched Michael, always with the fire in his eyes. *How did this pathetic angel get so good?* he thought.

Michael flew up, gaining altitude, while Satan exploded from the ground to chase after him.

Michael stopped flapping his wings rapidly, and folded one wing in to drop sideways at Satan who was far below. But Satan had a counter move, raising his empty hand he started to shoot flames up at Michael.

Michael had no such power, so he needed to get in close. He wrapped his other wing, this time diving at Satan. Flames whizzed by Michael.

Satan thought this was one of the most foolish moves he ever saw an angel do. And for an instant he felt he had caused it by making Michael afraid. He smiled proudly and continued to shoot flames at Michael.

One of the flames hit dead on Michael's sword, making its flames ignite with even greater brightness than the sun itself. This temporarily blinded Satan enough for Michael to hit him with his strongest downward slash. Satan fell with such speed that one was not sure whether it was a bolt of lightning or not. He left a trail of burning feathers as he plummeted to the plains with a tremendous force. His body smashed right onto the crack, and opened a hole into the unknown.

The sky swarmed with angels as shock ensued in the minds of Satan's troops. Losing hope, they retreated following Satan into the deep chasm.

Heaven's army cheered. Gabriel and Jahoel watched as Michael glided down to the edge of the chasm. Michael won, but at what cost? Looking around he saw hundreds of dead angels, their bodies not yet faded into oblivion.

CHAPTER V

Angels of the Crack

After the war was over, Michael decided to take a walk down the street. He felt relieved and redeemed, but there was only one thing that stood out in his mind—he wished that his friend Uriel could have been there with him. In a way he had; but no war, no fight, and not even a victory could fill the gap in his heart.

Michael walked down the street of the big city, and even though angels and humans knew him as the biggest hero, he was not satisfied by such things. Then, as he turned the corner he saw someone who looked just like Uriel.

"Hello my old friend," the angel said to him.

Still with a look of confusion on his face, Michael did not recognize him. It was probably the shock. And after being in an incredible war, the reality that Uriel could still be alive was even more incredible.

"Uriel?" Michael finally said.

"I've made it," Uriel said.

"Uriel!" Michael voiced as they hugged each other. "How can this be?"

"We are immortal, so we can not be gone forever," Uriel stated.

"I thought I would never see your face again," Michael said, "where were you?"

Uriel answered in a quiet thoughtful voice, "I was lost, it was an empty dark place, and there was no escape. My flaming sword was missing, so I could not use it to find my way. Flapping my wings for the longest time, I was beginning to lose all hope.

"To my surprise I saw a crack form in the ceiling far away from me. Someone fell through it, and then angels followed. That someone, though bruised, was Satan. His army had swords and did not look like a happy bunch, so I needed to get out. I realized they had been driven out of Heaven, and soon it was clear to them all, that this place would be their new home.

"When they saw me I knew I was in trouble, but just as they came at me, one of them turned with sword drawn. It was a women angel—she told me that it was time for us to get back to God. Her diversion got me the time I needed. After I made it to the crack, she herself fought her way out."

"What was her name?" Michael wondered.

"It was Sariel, one of your soldiers."

"Really?"

"Yes, Sariel changed armors to sneak in with the other side. She needed to find out the outcome of Satan's army."

"Well, she is to be commended," Michael said.

Uriel thought of how Sariel went back in there,

probably to rescue more angels that would soon appear there as well.

Just then Jahoel landed and walked over to them both.

"Michael, it is time," Jahoel said in a respectful voice.

Michael knew at once what this meant—it was time to meet with God. After all that had happened, only a meeting with God would set everything straight.

He flew with his sword ablaze as he had done before, but this time citizens below watched in awe as their hero went by, carrying his weapon, the one he used which saved the day. They all cheered.

Soon Michael entered the temple of God, swiftly he walked down the hallway to see the Lord, unsure what he might think of the prior battle. With sword still in hand, he knelt before the Lord Almighty. Spreading open his wings he laid the sword on the temple floor. He waited respectfully for the Lord's Judgment.

The Lord looked over at Michael and smiled.

"There is no need to worry my friend, you have served me well."

Michael looked up in surprise; to be called a friend by God was the greatest feeling. He stood up and folded his wings in.

"I do not need to judge you, because you are my friend," the Lord explained.

"I understand," Michael said, breaking a smile on his face that he tried to contain. All of the sudden, Michael understood that everything would be fine because the Lord would take care of it.

"Much has changed, now that Satan is gone. You are to be my highest Archangel now," the Lord explained.

"And what will become of Satan?" Michael asked.

"The dark place below the plains was a place untouched by my hand, Satan is free to make and do whatever he wishes there," said the Lord.

Michael wondered what Satan would do with it.

The Lord answered Michael's thoughts, "Satan shall rule all the fallen angels in a place of fire and rock. He shall be known as Lucifer, the Devil himself. The place shall be known as Hell, and his angels known as demons. The dark city of Gehenna will be in its center, and within it they will make a gate to Earth, much like our own. But most importantly whenever humans on Earth are evil and die, they shall be sent *there* from now on. A spokesmen from here must be sent, to tell them all of these changes."

"Who would that be . . . me?" Michael said.

"No, I need you and Uriel to guard the crack, and make sure no evil enters this place again. I will be sending Jesus to Earth instead," the Lord answered.

"Jesus, who is he?" Michael wondered.

"Jesus Christ is part of me, as is the Holy spirit. You see, he has always been here, you just did not see him," the Lord explained, "he was in the crowd when you left the streets, he was at the library when you were studying, and he was on the hill when you fought Satan."

Michael's eyes widened at such a thought.

"As a spokesman, the Christ will be a guide, a savior, and a redeemer. The word shall become flesh. Now that you know of him, you should bow your head in honor of him, for his name is greater than any angel's."

This seemed reasonable to Michael being that Jesus was a part of the Lord (who was his good friend).

Michael knelt down and lifted up his sword. He then left, with a new found respect for the Lord. Jesus, who was part of the Lord, would soon live the life of a human—he would be born like a man, and he would feel pain, sorrow, and anguish. He thought about it so deeply he said out loud, "I will do whatever I can to help you." Then he exited the temple and saw Uriel standing just outside.

"Well then, help me understand this," Uriel said as if Michael's words were directed at him, "I heard that you defeated Satan. How did you do this?"

"Uriel, I just did what you told me to. I went to the library," responded Michael.

Uriel looked down and smiled. "Yes, I should go there more often." Then he looked up at Michael.

Michael then announced to Uriel, "We must stop those demons from entering back through that crack. Are you with me?"

"You bet," Uriel said, pulling out his sword to clash with Michael's (this was a brotherly gesture). "We are strong and we must always uphold the weak."

Then they both shot off into the sky with swords drawn, so that there would always be peace in a place where there was meant to be peace; and as long as there were those to take up destiny's call, they would be there to fight for it.

ANGEL COMPENDIUM

(In order of mention)

Michael: Angel of truth, and protector of the just. A seemingly ordinary angel, who does not realize his great potential.

Gabriel: Responsible and beautiful. She is an angel of hope and life.

Uriel: Angel of music and literature, with the gift to transform disappointments.

Satan: Leader of the angels, but something seems a little off about him.

Zephon: Good at finding hidden things. He was put in charge of the Heavenly Library.

Jahoel: The messenger of God. He is also in charge of the Child School in Heaven.

Azael: Guardian of hidden treasures before his mischief lead to much destruction and chaos.

Raphael: Angel of healing and courage.

Raziel: Angel book author and chief of supreme mysteries.

Gallizur: Teacher of wisdom and protector of angels.

Zadkiel: Angel of memory, benevolence, and human spiritual growth.

Arcan: King of the air angels.

Oriel: Angel of twilight, destiny, and guardian of children.

Mediat: Angel of communication and friendship.

Sariel: An angel of healing and of death that retrieved the soul of Moses.

About the Author

J.S. MILIK is a Second Degree Black Belt in Traditional Taekwon-do, giving him an experienced background in telling fight scenes for stories. He has been a Christian all his life, and has studied Angel Lore and Ancient History. He belonged to the Fencing Team in both High School and College. Mr. Milik has also published Poetry and took college courses in Web Design, Programming, Writing, and Art.